Days With Frog and Toad

by Arnold Lobel

HarperCollins*Publishers*

For Liz Gordon

HarperCollins®, 🍂®, and I Can Read Book® are trademarks of HarperCollins Publishers Inc.
A portion of this book previously appeared in *Cricket*.

Manufactured in China. For information address HarperCollins Children's Books, a division of HarperCollins Publishers, 10 East 53rd Street, New York, NY 10022. www.harpercollinschildrens.com

Library of Congress Cataloging-in-Publication Data
Lobel, Arnold.
    Days with Frog and Toad.
    (An I can read book)
    Summary: Frog and Toad spend their days together, but find sometimes it's nice to be alone.
    [1. Frogs—Fiction.   2. Toads—Fiction.   3. Friendship—Fiction.]   I. Title.
PZ7.L7795Day   [E]   78-21786
ISBN-10: 0-06-023963-8 — ISBN-13: 978-0-06-023963-3
ISBN-10: 0-06-023964-6 (lib. bdg.) — ISBN-13: 978-0-06-023964-0 (lib. bdg.)
ISBN-10: 0-06-444058-3 (pbk.) — ISBN-13: 978-0-06-444058-5 (pbk.)

09 10 11 12 13 SCP 20 19
❖

Contents

Tomorrow

Toad woke up.

"Drat!" he said.

"This house is a mess.

I have so much work to do."

Frog looked through the window.

"Toad, you are right,"

said Frog. "It is a mess."

Toad pulled the covers

over his head.

"I will do it tomorrow,"

said Toad.

"Today I will take life easy."

Frog came into the house.

"Toad," said Frog,

"your pants and jacket

are lying on the floor."

"Tomorrow," said Toad

from under the covers.

"Your kitchen sink

is filled with dirty dishes,"

said Frog.

"Tomorrow," said Toad.

"There is dust on your chairs."

"Tomorrow," said Toad.

"Your windows need scrubbing,"
said Frog.

"Your plants need watering."

"Tomorrow!" cried Toad.

"I will do it all tomorrow!"

Toad sat on the edge

of his bed.

"Blah," said Toad.

"I feel down in the dumps."

"Why?" asked Frog.

"I am thinking

about tomorrow,"

said Toad.

"I am thinking about

all of the many things

that I will have to do."

"Yes," said Frog,

"tomorrow will be

a very hard day for you."

"But Frog," said Toad,
"if I pick up my pants
and jacket right now,
then I will not have to
pick them up tomorrow, will I?"
"No," said Frog.
"You will not have to."
Toad picked up his clothes.
He put them in the closet.

"Frog," said Toad,

"if I wash my dishes right now,

then I will not have to

wash them tomorrow, will I?"

"No," said Frog.

"You will not have to."

Toad washed and dried his dishes.

He put them in the cupboard.

"Frog," said Toad,

"if I dust my chairs

and scrub my windows

and water my plants right now,

then I will not have to

do it tomorrow, will I?"

"No," said Frog. "You will not

have to do any of it."

Toad dusted
his chairs.

He scrubbed
his windows.

He watered
his plants.

"There,"

said Toad.

"Now I feel better.

I am not

in the dumps anymore."

"Why?" asked Frog.

"Because I have done

all that work," said Toad.

"Now I can save tomorrow

for something that I really want to do."

"What is that?" asked Frog.

14

"Tomorrow," said Toad,

"I can just take life easy."

Toad went back to bed.

He pulled the covers

over his head

and fell asleep.

The Kite

Frog and Toad went out
to fly a kite.
They went to
a large meadow
where the wind was strong.
"Our kite will fly up and up,"
said Frog.
"It will fly all the way up
to the top of the sky."

"Toad," said Frog,

"I will hold the ball of string.

You hold the kite and run."

Toad ran across the meadow.

He ran as fast as his short legs
could carry him.

The kite went up in the air.

It fell to the ground with a bump.

Toad heard laughter.

Three robins were sitting in a bush.

"That kite will not fly,"
said the robins.
"You may as well give up."

Toad ran back to Frog.
"Frog," said Toad,
"this kite will not fly.
I give up."

"We must make a second try,"
said Frog.
"Wave the kite over your head.
Perhaps that will make it fly."

Toad ran back across the meadow.
He waved the kite over his head.

The kite went up in the air
and then fell down with a thud.
"What a joke!" said the robins.
"That kite will never
get off the ground."

Toad ran back to Frog.

"This kite is a joke," he said.

"It will never get off the ground."

"We have to make

a third try," said Frog.

"Wave the kite over your head

and jump up and down.

Perhaps that will make it fly."

Toad ran across
the meadow again.
He waved the kite
over his head.
He jumped up and down.
The kite went up in the air
and crashed down into the grass.
"That kite is junk,"
said the robins.
"Throw it away and go home."

Toad ran back to Frog.

"This kite is junk," he said.

"I think we should

throw it away and go home."

"Toad," said Frog,

"we need one more try.

Wave the kite over your head.

Jump up and down

and shout UP KITE UP."

Toad ran across the meadow.

He waved the kite over his head.

He jumped up and down.

He shouted, "UP KITE UP!"

The kite flew into the air.

It climbed higher and higher.

"We did it!" cried Toad.

"Yes," said Frog.

"If a running try

did not work,

and a running and waving try

did not work,

and a running, waving,

and jumping try

did not work,

I knew that

a running, waving, jumping,

and shouting try

just had to work."

The robins flew out of the bush.

But they could not fly

as high as the kite.

Frog and Toad sat

and watched their kite.

It seemed to be flying

way up at the top of the sky.

Shivers

The night was cold and dark.

"Listen to the wind

howling in the trees," said Frog.

"What a fine time for a ghost story."

Toad moved deeper into his chair.

"Toad," asked Frog,

"don't you like to be scared?

Don't you like to feel the shivers?"

"I am not too sure," said Toad.

Frog made a fresh pot of tea.

He sat down

and began a story.

"When I was small," said Frog,

"my mother and father and I

went out for a picnic.

On the way home we lost our way.

My mother was worried.

'We must get home,' she said.

'We do not want to meet

the Old Dark Frog.'

'Who is that?' I asked.

'A terrible ghost,'

said my father.

'He comes out at night and eats

little frog children for supper.'"

Toad sipped his tea.

"Frog," he asked,

"are you making this up?"

"Maybe yes and maybe no,"

said Frog.

"My mother and father
went to search for a path,"
said Frog.
"They told me to wait
until they came back.
I sat under a tree and waited.
The woods became dark.
I was afraid.
Then I saw two huge eyes.
It was the Old Dark Frog.

32

He was standing near me."

"Frog," asked Toad,

"did this really happen?"

"Maybe it did

and maybe it didn't,"

said Frog.

Frog went on with the story.

"The Dark Frog pulled

a jump rope out of his pocket.

'I am not hungry now,'
said the Dark Frog.
'I have eaten too many
tasty frog children.
But after I jump rope
one hundred times,
I will be hungry again.
Then I will eat YOU!' "

"The Dark Frog tied one end

of the rope to a tree.

'Turn for me!' he shouted.

I turned the rope for the Dark Frog.

He jumped twenty times.

'I am beginning to get hungry,'

said the Dark Frog.

He jumped fifty times.

'I am getting hungrier,'

said the Dark Frog.

He jumped ninety times.

'I am very hungry now!'

said the Dark Frog."

"What happened then?"

asked Toad.

"I had to save my life,"

said Frog.

"I ran around

and around the tree

with the rope.

I tied up

the Old Dark Frog.

He roared and screamed.

I ran away fast."

"I found my mother and father,"
said Frog.

"We came safely home."

"Frog," asked Toad,
"was that a true story?"
"Maybe it was
and maybe it wasn't,"
said Frog.

Frog and Toad sat
close by the fire.
They were scared.
The teacups shook
in their hands.
They were having the shivers.
It was a good, warm feeling.

The Hat

On Toad's birthday

Frog gave him a hat.

Toad was delighted.

"Happy birthday," said Frog.

Toad put on the hat.

It fell down over his eyes.

"I am sorry," said Frog.

"That hat is much too big for you.

I will give you something else."

"No," said Toad. "This hat
is your present to me. I like it.
I will wear it the way it is."

43

Frog and Toad went for a walk.

Toad tripped over a rock.

He bumped into a tree.

He fell in a hole.

"Frog," said Toad,

"I can't see anything.

I will not be able to wear

your beautiful present.

This is a sad birthday for me."

Frog and Toad
were sad
for a while.
Then Frog said,

"Toad, here is what you must do.

Tonight when you go to bed

you must think

some very big thoughts.

Those big thoughts will make

your head grow larger.

In the morning

your new hat may fit."

"What a good idea," said Toad.

That night when Toad went to bed
he thought the biggest thoughts
that he could think.
Toad thought about
giant sunflowers.
He thought about tall oak trees.
He thought about high mountains
covered with snow.

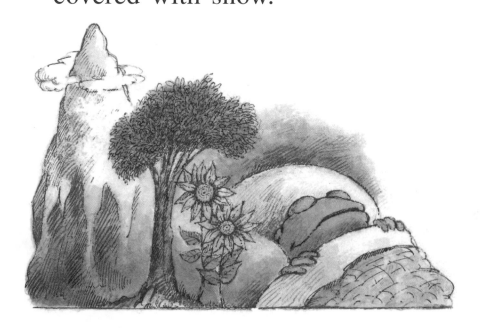

Then Toad fell asleep.

Frog came into Toad's house.

He came in quietly.

Frog found the hat

and took it to his house.

Frog poured some water on the hat.

He put the hat

in a warm place to dry.

It began to shrink.

That hat grew smaller and smaller.

Frog went back to Toad's house.

Toad was still fast asleep.

Frog put the hat back on the hook

where he found it.

When Toad woke up in the morning,

he put the hat on his head.

It was just the right size.

Toad ran to Frog's house.

"Frog, Frog!" he cried.

"All those big thoughts

have made my head

much larger.

Now I can wear your present!"

Frog and Toad went for a walk.

Toad did not trip

over a rock.

He did not bump into a tree.

He did not fall

in a hole.

It turned out to be

a very pleasant

day after Toad's birthday.

Alone

Toad went to Frog's house.

He found a note on the door.

The note said,

"Dear Toad, I am not at home.

I went out.

I want to be alone."

"Alone?" said Toad.

"Frog has me for a friend.

Why does he want to be alone?"

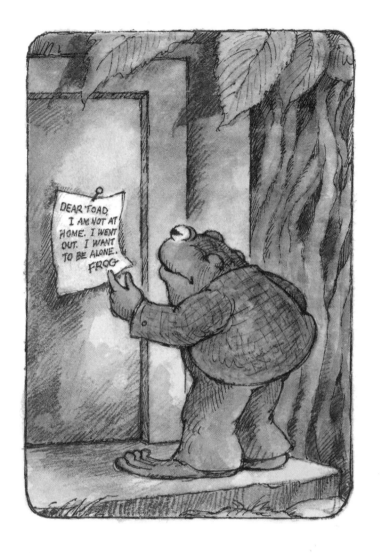

Toad looked through the windows.

He looked in the garden.

He did not see Frog.

Toad went to the woods.

Frog was not there.

He went to the meadow.

Frog was not there.

Toad went down to the river.

There was Frog.

He was sitting on an island
by himself.

"Poor Frog," said Toad.

"He must be very sad.

I will cheer him up."

Toad ran home.

He made sandwiches.

He made a pitcher of iced tea.

He put everything

in a basket.

Toad hurried

back to the river.

"Frog," he shouted,

"it's me.

It's your best friend, Toad!"

Frog was too far away to hear.

Toad took off his jacket

and waved it like a flag.

Frog was too far away to see.

Toad shouted and waved,

but it was no use.

Frog sat on the island.

He did not see or hear Toad.

A turtle swam by.

Toad climbed on the turtle's back.

"Turtle," said Toad,

"carry me to the island.

Frog is there.

He wants to be alone."

"If Frog wants to be alone,"

said the turtle,

"why don't you leave him alone?"

"Maybe you are right," said Toad.

"Maybe Frog does not

want to see me.

Maybe he does not want me

to be his friend anymore."

"Yes, maybe," said the turtle

as he swam to the island.

"Frog!" cried Toad.

"I am sorry for all

the dumb things I do.

I am sorry for all

the silly things I say.

Please be my friend again!"

Toad slipped off the turtle.

With a splash, he fell in the river.

Frog pulled Toad

up onto the island.

Toad looked in the basket.

The sandwiches were wet.

The pitcher of iced tea was empty.

"Our lunch is spoiled," said Toad.

"I made it for you, Frog,

so that you would be happy."

"But Toad," said Frog.

"I *am* happy. I am very happy.

This morning

when I woke up

I felt good because

the sun was shining.

I felt good because

I was a frog.

And I felt good because

I have you for a friend.

I wanted to be alone.

I wanted to think about

how fine everything is."

"Oh," said Toad.

"I guess that is a very good reason

for wanting to be alone."

"Now," said Frog,

"I will be glad *not* to be alone.

Let's eat lunch."

Frog and Toad

stayed on the island

all afternoon.

They ate wet sandwiches

without iced tea.

They were two close friends

sitting alone together.